T0380955

Key to Chivalry

Fairy Tale with Teacher and Parenting Social Emotional Learning Skills

Monica Nicoll, Ph.D., LCMHC

Illustrator: Leslie Beauregard

To order additional copies of this book, contact:
Xlibris
1-888-795-4274
www.Xlibris.com
Orders@Xlibris.com

Key to Chivalry

Fairy Tale with Teacher and Parenting Social Emotional Learning Skills

Monica Nicoll, Ph.D., LCMHC

Dear _____

I value every moment with you. I have lovingly watched you grow up and have learned so much about you and how you see your world. We read this book together and even shared it with your teacher.

_____

_____

_____

_____

_____

_____

Love,

Mom or Dad

Your picture

_____

Squire

Thomas stirred. It was very early in the morning as he gazed out the window. There was only a faint light. The sun was barely peeking out from the shadows of the morning. He wondered why he felt like tiny squirrels were running in his tummy. What was he thinking about?

Thomas brushed a blonde curl from his forehead as he sat up and stretched. "Ah", he thought, "I start my knight training today".

He imagined all the big strong knights that he saw yesterday with large muscles and smooth moves. He looked at his tiny muscles, flexed a little, and wondered how he was going to keep up with them. Chow, his black kitten, purred at his feet. "How easy was life for a kitten?" asked Thomas as he gazed at Chow snuggled into his soft quilt. "Pretty cozy", Thomas thought. Chow yawned and stretched lazily.

Thomas sighed deeply.

Thomas thought about his new journey of becoming a knight filled with only his dreams.

Aspects
of
Training

Thomas was the son of a strong medieval knight. He had been serving as a page in a lord's castle for the past year. He patiently waited for his dream to come true; to become a Knight! Now he would finally learn the skills of horsemanship, archery, jousting, swordsmanship, and team work. Most importantly, he would also learn the oath of chivalry and knighthood!

Thomas looked forward to training his strength, fitness, and skills with various weapons. Last year, he had spent much time tending to the knight's horse, cleaning the stables, polishing the knight's armor, and maintaining his weapons. "Ugh", Thomas thought, "some of those tasks were a little boring".

But, now he would learn the chivalric codes of conduct. He would listen to famous tales of Arthur, Percival, and Lancelot. His dreams were filled with excitement! He could see himself on the white horse riding in the parade of knights. He imagined the soft feel of the horse's mane and the wind on his cheeks.

In Knight's school, Thomas learned the oath he must live by every day. The words danced on the page. Thomas felt warm in his chest. He thought deeply about how he must live by these ideas. This code would shape his decisions and actions. Knowing these values gave Thomas a sense of peace. Thomas learned that with one's word, one's actions must also follow. The Code of Chivalry means one must act as one speaks. He printed the Code on his tapestry.

- Faith
- Charity
- Justice
- Wisdom
- Forethought
- Temperance

- Resolution
- Truth
- Liberality
- Diligence
- Hope
- Valor

Code of Chivalry

I, Thomas promise

To serve the liege trainer in valor and faith

To protect the weak and defenseless

To give help to widows and orphans, the needy, everyone one actually

To refrain from the wanton giving of offence

To live by honor and for glory

To despise financial reward

To fight for the welfare of all

To help those placed in authority

To guard the honor of fellow knights

To eschew unfairness, meanness and deceit

To keep faith

At all times to speak the truth

To persevere to the end in any enterprise begun

To respect the honor of women, and all peoples

Never to refuse a challenge from an equal

Never to turn thy back upon a foe.

The birds chirped and the wind rustled softly through the trees. The fluffy clouds touched and formed into ever changing shapes. Thomas peered upwards and felt the wind touch his cold cheeks. These squirrels were back in his tummy. He felt his heart beat a little faster.

The new squires all gathered in the courtyard as the master Knight began to give his daily lesson. The first task was horsemanship. The horse neighed and swished his tail. The teacher lifted Thomas onto the horse; this was really high. His little legs dangled in the stirrups. The horse would not move for Thomas. He just stayed in place as if Thomas was not even on him. A huge lump fell into his tummy. Thomas thought he heard the other squire's laughter.

The next hour was swordsmanship. The sword weighed a ton. They practiced with wood swords first. He practiced the moves and counter-moves. He was shown how to block and twirl the sword. But then, his foot caught a hole and down he fell onto the ground. The other squires laughed loudly at Thomas as he struggled.

Anya helped him up and just smiled with her warmth and kindness; but Thomas still felt a heavy sadness. It had been a difficult day. The laughter echoed in his ears for hours afterward. The day ended with a long run. Thomas struggled to keep up and his breath was labored. His little thin legs felt the pain of his struggles. The evergreen trees seemed to sigh as he passed. It was as if they could feel his heavy heart.

That night when Thomas went to sleep, the Dragon came into his thoughts.

The Dragon filled him with negative thoughts. The Dragon told him "he could not do the things others could do, that he was weak, and that he did not belong with the others. I can't, I can't, and I can't do things well…" He could not sleep and his Dragon thoughts swirled in his mind. Big tears rolled down his little cheeks. His heart ached. Chow, his kitten, looked on with big eyes and sweet purrs. "If only you could know how I feel", sighed Thomas, as he sadly hugged kitty. Chow's fur felt soft and warm.

With his heavy heart, Thomas trudged onward to his class the next day. He decided to watch Anya and see how she handled her training. After many hours, Thomas noticed that Anya did not do everything perfectly. But, she kept going no matter what! She tried again and again at a skill. She never seemed to get discouraged. She made little adjustments to her hands, feet, positions. Anya's courage and determination seemed to make a difference to her learning.

At the end of the day Thomas walked over to her and asked how she kept on trying. Anya glanced around and when no one was listening, she said, "I keep my wise mind with me at all times; the wise Owl is my guide and teaches me positive thoughts." Thomas was intrigued. Where could he find his wise Owl thoughts and his wise mind?

Anya led him to a thick set of trees after practice. There the majestic Owl emerged and his wings hugged Anya and whispered a word of support to her. The Owl then turned to Thomas and said, "You could use some wise mind thoughts, I can see it from your sad face." With that, he hugged Thomas and told him to "always believe in yourself, let the Dragon thoughts go. Be content with wherever you are with a new skill. It takes time to learn and there is no room for Dragon thoughts". The Owl told Thomas to close his eyes and picture himself struggling. "Feel your feelings", Owl said. The Owl hugged his warm wings around Thomas and whispered, "See yourself getting up, see yourself in your mind's eye doing the skill well, feel the warmth of my wings, believe in yourself and your ability to practice and do things well over time. Let your stumbling moments go into the breeze". Thomas heart felt warm as little happy squirrels bounced in his tummy and he relaxed. Thomas breathed deeply letting the warm feeling surround him.

Anya had shown such caring as she helped him and shared the Owl. Anya was chivalry in action.

Thomas banished the Dragon and his negative thinking out to the forest. Thomas took charge of himself. He felt warm in his heart and hopeful. He hugged the Owl and started to love his own wise mind. He knew he belonged no matter what and that over time he could always do a little better each and every day. "It is where I am", thought Thomas, "Not where others are in their skills that matters. I am doing the best I can. I matter and I can love myself no matter what is happening", declared Thomas.

Several nights later, while the moon shone over his bed and the wind billowed through the trees, Thomas suddenly felt sad for the Dragon. He might be lonely out in the woods, he thought. He peered out the window. The moon had wrapped a warm cloud around itself bringing shadows to the ground.

Thomas took the Owl and went to find the Dragon. They found Dragon sitting with sad eyes and a heavy heart. Thomas felt pain in his heart too when he saw the Dragon. It is sad to feel unwanted no matter who we are. Everyone has feelings. Everyone deserves to be loved. Thomas hugged the Dragon. Tears welled in their eyes. Thomas wanted to help both with Dragon and himself. With the help of the Owl's wise mind, Thomas invited Dragon to think a worry thought and then, quickly change into a positive, hopeful thought; a solution thought. Dragon also had good things to offer. Like be careful, think realistically, and watch your step. "Too much worry or stewing in our negative thinking takes up time and leads to being discouraged", whispered Owl. With a little work, Dragon could learn to use both his wise mind and his positive Dragon mind. Dragon basked in the joy of feeling accepted. Dragon started coming to the training grounds with Thomas, Owl, and Anya. Little changes in our thinking and kindness can make a difference to how someone feels. Everyone belongs.

After many moons went by, Thomas awoke to a new worry thought. It was about his Knight test later that day and all his hard work and training. Those squirrels were back in his tummy. Fear thoughts roamed freely. "What if I can't do it, what if I fall, what if people laugh at me, what if I drop my sword". Thomas breathed deeply and listened to his breath. He invited his Owl wise mind thoughts into his mind. "I am ok, I'll be ok. I'll do the best I can for today. I believe in me and all my hard work. I trust myself. I will let my fear go to the wind today". He quickly added, "I will let go of worry about how I will do in the end or how I want it to go. Instead, I will give it my best. Let's see how it goes; let the chips fall where they may". "I'll trust my muscles to do what they have been taught in all my practice." Thomas sighed loudly and breathed slowly.

Hours before his test, Thomas saw his neighbor, Mrs. Gray, struggling with her groceries. Thomas remembered how Anya had helped him. Thomas loved how he felt when he helped Dragon. So he quickly ran to Mrs. Gray's side and helped her load the big sacks into her cart. With glowing eyes, she thanked Thomas for his help. Her horse neighed gently as if nodding in agreement with his kindness. Thomas' heart felt warm after helping her. "We can all help each other to make life easier. It sure feels good to help others", thought Thomas.

The moment had arrived for his test. Thomas picked up his sword and wielded his movements. He let his muscles work as they had been trained. Next, Thomas jumped on his horse and worked well with his horse just as he had trained. His archery also went well as he relaxed, breathed deep and steadied his hands. He shot between breathes and remained calm. The five squires then worked together in a pattern. In this way, their swords protected each other. In the group, Anya stumbled and dropped her sword. Thomas picked it up and whispered "keep going and keep your Owl thoughts". Anya smiled her knowing smile, she really did believe in herself. This was true companionship; they had each other's backs. Chivalry means caring about others, helping each other and knowing what another needs.

Many years before Thomas, after months of training, a squire would go through a dubbing ceremony. Early on the ceremony was just a small, open-handed pat to the neck followed by a stern warning to conduct himself with courage and loyalty.

For Thomas and his group of squires, the King would use their swords to knight them by tapping on their shoulders. Thomas passed his test! He kneeled in the King's presence and Thomas received his Knighthood distinction and his Valyrian sword. Anya passed too.

Thomas stood with Owl and Dragon. His new sword gleamed in the sunshine. The evergreens proudly bowed in the breeze at Thomas. Chow purred loudly in the background. Dreams can come true if one believes in oneself.

Learning and Discussion Section

For Teachers and Parents

Thomas thinks about his upcoming day where he is learning to be a knight. His dreams are lit up and his energy is charged. Coupled with the thought that he does not know how to do his new skills, he immediately thinks about the idea that he may not do well. This creates a reaction in his body and it feels like squirrels in his tummy. This is fear. His worry thoughts, his feelings, make his body react. We can physically feel our feelings in our bodies.

Parent and Teacher Key Focus

Concepts:

Anticipation, dreams, nerves, fear, new skills

Learning:

Have each child draw their dreams. Share your dreams, teacher or parent; what steps did you use to make them happen?

Have each child with your help find the steps they need to get to their dreams.

Draw each step and identify what each step needs.

Identify squirrels in your child's tummy: what fears or worries do they have; what do they need to know to feel belief in their dreams?

Thomas has been patient over the last few years while he worked up to his time where his knight training began. Mundane tasks develop persistence, patience, and a time to believe in yourself. Thomas dares to dream and dream big… can you find your dreams?

Parent and Teacher Key Focus

Identify that every day we learn and that we are filling our minds and bodies with positive qualities.

What stood out today? What made you feel today? How? What tasks may not be so exciting but continue to make you grow and learn?

Word and deed, values, who do you intend to be, can people tell your intentions by your actions?

❊ Faith	❊ Resolution
❊ Charity	❊ Truth
❊ Justice	❊ Liberality
❊ Wisdom	❊ Diligence
❊ Forethought	❊ Hope
❊ Temperance	❊ Valor

The above virtues are featured in the Code of Chivalry.

Parent and Teacher Key Focus

Learning:

What are your and your family's commitments, words to live by, and your code of chivalry?

How do we help each other in our family or classroom?

Discuss how in your family or class, we act like we speak; if we say we are here to help each other then we live by helping each other.

The beginning of skill development does not bode well for Thomas. He falls and is not able to make his horse move. His legs are weary and he struggles with running and moving well. The beginning of skill development is the most crucial for self-kindness and compassion of others. The body and mind need time to develop and muscle memory development takes time. Everyone develops at a different pace.

Every day there is opportunity to learn new things. When we do not know how to do things it can feel scary or make us unsure of ourselves. We lose faith and trust in our abilities when we have not given ourselves time to learn. The learning curve is a place where we are as we develop skills. With encouraged practice, we will move around the learning curve to mastery. With judgement, we will 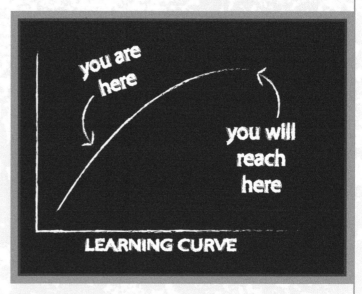 negatively affect our minds and our bodies. This impedes learning and slows our minds down. Finding ways to improve by asking questions and watching others that can do a skill will help us find ways to learn and move around the learning curve. Mastery of a skill will feel fluid, flowing, and natural. The question for skill development is, "why not you".

Parent and Teacher Key Focus

Concepts:

Persistence, shaping, chunking down, visualization, learning curve disappointment, judgment, high expectations, courage

Learning curve: take time to let your muscles learn

Have each child identify where they are on the learning curve. Stay in courage and keep practicing; a little each day moves the child around the learning curve. Make little steps toward success; chunking down a skill to manageable steps.

Teach visualization, imagine doing the skill and doing it well; love yourself always

Does anyone have high expectations for you? Draw or talk about how you feel and where the person wants you to be. You can only be where you are and be at peace with your thoughts. No pressure

Disappointment is a natural feeling when things do not go well. Feeling disappointed or sad is ok, judging yourself is not ok. Being on the learning curve ought to be just that; there is much pressure to be great right away. We can watch others and compare ourselves. When someone learns faster or has worked on a skill before, they may be smoother and seem more able. Dragon thoughts or negative thinking can become a side effect of disappointment. Disappointment could be a feeling that is accompanied by strategic planning for how to solve the issue. Strategic planning is putting into place areas of improvement, new alignment of positions, corrections of arms, legs, and body, and also allowing time of practice. Not believing in yourself because you cannot do something creates tension in our bodies. These dragon thoughts can become a habit which leads to patterns of being unkind to yourself. Dragon thoughts and negative thinking patterns will not improve skills.

Parent and Teacher Key Focus

Concepts:

Dragon thoughts, negative thinking, monkey chatter, physiology
Identify your monkey chatter; is the monkey negative or "I can" mindset?

Where does your child feel their worry? Their fear?
Identify 4 strengths that the child has.

Have each child identify a safe place in their world; their bed with a cozy blanket, a soft dog's fur to snuggle with, a warm arm around their backs when the day is tough.

Thinking positive thoughts, owl wise mind thinking, allows one to believe in oneself. The "I can do it" belief. When we have learned a skill and it does not work well, we can doubt ourselves and our abilities. Early memory reconstruction can help.

Visualize the Early memory moments where we experienced a difficult time; the memory will pop into your mind… reconstruct the memory to see us doing well, wrapping the Owl's wings around us, asking for what we need, and doing the skill well. Apply the new learning and trust in ourselves to the skill of today. Practice visualization which is seeing ourselves doing the skill well over and over in our imagination. This allows our minds to practice doing a skill well. We all have the capacity for negative and positive thinking. our private logic

Parent and Teacher Key Focus

Concepts:

Skill mastery, shaping changes in positions toward mastery, Owl thinking, visualization, ER reconstruction, mindfulness

Learning:

Time and practice makes skills improve. Describe your practice routine in school, in the field, or in your activity. Mindfulness is the focusing on one's awareness on the present moment, while calmly acknowledging and accepting one's feelings, thoughts, and bodily sensations.

Early memory reconstruction: Feel the feeling and remember where you first felt this feeling. Was there a negative experience you can remember? These memories become part of your thinking. By examining the first experience, we can hug ourselves and tell ourselves what we needed in the first experience. Sometimes we hold onto thoughts that do not serve our practice. Let them go and rework being able to practice freely.

What is your positive thinking/Owl thinking? What are the thoughts that make you feel good and hopeful?

Thomas pushes Dragon and his negative thinking out of him and into the forest. This is a good way to get rid of negative judgmental thinking. You cannot think positively and negatively at the same time. Give yourself a chance to learn a little each day. We do learn every day. We also belong without having to do everything perfectly or to do anything at all. We all deserve to be a part of our lives and to matter. We have worth just because we are!

Parent and Teacher Key Focus

Concepts:

Banishing dragon, banishing negative thinking, refocus

Learning:

Comparing to others can give us negative feelings. Describe feeling worried about other's accomplishments or things they can do? It is ok to be happy for others but not ok to compare and make yourself feel less than.

Stop, drop and roll. Stop negative thinking in its tracks, drop the negative, and roll to positive and hopefulness. You can!

Refocusing means being in your calm mind; Good problem solving and right solutions come when we are in our wise owl mind. Talk things over when everyone is calm. There is a solution for everything.

Thomas tunes into his empathy and caring feelings. Caring about how others feel is good Knight behavior and part of chivalry. Do you think of how others feel and think about how others may feel when they are being left out? Dragon was sad and lonely being by himself with no one around to care. He made it harder on himself by being negative. Do you know someone that is negative or says negative things a lot? This person can be discouraged and does not know other ways to relate to people. Everyone can learn. Everyone can learn to re-think their old ways of negative thinking and find positive ways to connect. With positive Owl thinking, Dragon became a nice part of the group. This made him feel good too.

Parent and Teacher Key Focus

Concepts:

Empathy, empathy action, letting go putting negative into the wind to be carried away

Learning:

Describe a time where you helped someone.

At the end of the day ask your little ones who they helped today?

How did it feel to help someone?

In your imagination, picture a hot air balloon; put the negative experience, negative thoughts in the hot air balloon and let it go.

Little squirrels in your tummy are ok as long as they come along with good thoughts of "I can do". Those are your nerves; your feelings in your body. Big squirrels, guppy breathing or shallow breathing, beating heart, and sweating, are signs that there is too much arousal in your body. Too much arousal hampers your muscles from doing their jobs. By deep breathing, breathing counting in for 4 and out for 4, seeing yourself in your mind's eye imagining you doing the skill well, will give you a good feeling and capableness. Tune into expectations. Are you carrying your parent's expectations, your coaches', your teachers'? See yourself doing your skill. Then let go of how it will all turn out and let the day roll on. It is this moment that you have done your best for now. Let that be ok. Breathe deeply.

Note your monkey chatter or your noise in your brain. Listen to what you say when you are doing things. Bring Owl in and wrap yourself in positive thinking. I can do my best.

Parent and Teacher Key Focus

Concepts:

Nerves, monkey chatter, thinking informs our bodies, arousal levels, relaxed breathing, visualization

Learning:

Breathing for Calm. Take 10 minutes each day to practice breathing focus, count to 4 inhale and count to 4 exhale. Feel your heart rate slow down. Breathe in calm; breathe out worry.

Teach visualization by each student seeing themselves do their skills from start to finish. Make sure that they are positively finishing their skills.

Teach body scanning. From feet to the top of your head, allow each body part to relax, slow your breathing; let go of all thoughts and worry; be in the moment.

By deep breathing, calming can over the body. Too high expectations, perceived parent pressures, or trying to prove yourself can lead to increased arousal levels where your body can feel jittery, stiff muscles, and shaky in your chest. It is ok to be excited. Too much can make your skills difficult. Breathe deep, visualize, and focus on letting go of the end result. Just do.

Chivalry means helping and honoring others. Thomas helps Mrs. Gray and there is great warmth in our hearts when we help others. Having kindness and empathy is a good Knight skill as we understand that everyone may struggle. It can feel wonderful having someone understand our feelings and take the time to know what we really need. Notice others around you. Imagine how they are feeling. Always stay tuned to how you are feeling. Know what you need!

Thomas puts his practice and courage into his test. He lets all expectations go and trusts in his muscle memory and hard work. He breathes deep and tries his best. There is such a warmhearted feeling when you accomplish your dreams. It is your dream. Where you are with a skill is as far as you have learned. Stay focused on your practice only…

A ceremony or celebration can be big or small. Take a moment each day to acknowledge what you can do and something that you did today that made you feel warm inside and special. Let the warmth wash over and through you. Feel the warm feeling in your heart. You deserve to feel good.

Parent and Teacher Key Focus

Concepts:

Encouragement, ceremonies, special events in your family, kindness toward others, catching students helping others or making positive choices

Learning:

What made you feel special in your day today?

What is your favorite memory in your life so far?

What surprises you in your day at times?

What did you like that your teacher, Mom or Dad, or friend did today?

What encouraging words do you say to Mom or Dad or friends or teacher? Or do they say to you?

Identify your dreams and how it feels when they happen.

What are special events or traditions that you and your family or a friend's family do?

What are encouraging words that you enjoy hearing from your teacher or your parent or your coach?

Personal Coat of Arms

During battle, the leader could hold up the coat of arms so the knights knew where to gather with their clansmen. Each leader developed his own unique coat of arms which reflected things about his family, to which king or clan he was loyal to and something unique about his family. Draw in each section of the coat of arms: something special about your family; one thing you do or enjoy the best; something special about you; something in your dreams; the best thing you ever did; something you feel is important to you or your family; your favorite school subject. At the bottom, write what your family stands for with your Mom or Dad or family member.

Love, listen, laugh, and practice..

Concepts:

* anticipation- the act of looking forward
* arousal levels-to stimulate to action or to bodily readiness for activity
* banishing dragon putting negative thoughts away/ pushing dragon out to the woods
* catching students helping others-social interest; focusing on students helpfulness
* ceremonies- a formal act or series of acts prescribed by ritual, protocol, or convention
* chunking down-breaks up long strings of information into units or chunks. The resulting chunks are easier to commit to memory; physical skills made easier by small increments
* courage-mental or moral strength to venture, persevere, and withstand danger, fear, or difficulty
* disappointment-defeated in expectation or hope
* dragon thoughts-negative thinking; pessimism
* dreams-a strongly desired goal or purpose
* early recollection reconstruction-are stories of single, specific incidents in childhood which the individual is able to reconstitute in present experience as mental images or as focused sensory memories; reconstructing and healing the direction of the memory
* empathy-the action of understanding, being aware of, being sensitive to, and vicariously experiencing the feelings, thoughts, and experience of another
* empathy action-upon feeling and being aware of another's feelings, putting action in response
* encouragement-to inspire with courage, spirit, or hope; to give help or patronage to
* fear-an unpleasant often strong emotion caused by anticipation or awareness of danger
* high expectations-having overly high expectations and a low view of self and one's needs; having perfectionistic expectations
* judgment-the process of forming an opinion or evaluation
* kindness toward others-element of empathy and caring; giving and caring for others; social interest
* learning curve- a curve plotting performance against practice; the course of progress made in learning something; take time to let your muscles learn

❋ learning curve disappointment-judging prior to giving time for the body/mind to learn

❋ letting go; putting negative into the wind to be carried away-letting go of negative by letting the thought go into the wind

❋ making positive choices-directed or moving toward a source of stimulation

❋ mindfulness-the practice of maintaining a nonjudgmental state of heightened or complete awareness of one's thoughts, emotions, or experiences on a moment-to-moment basis

❋ monkey chatter-constant chatter of the mind as monkey mind

❋ negative thinking-a thought process where people tend to find the worst in everything, or reduce their expectations by considering the worst possible scenarios

❋ nerves-nervous agitation or irritability

❋ new skills- the ability to use one's knowledge effectively and readily in execution or performance; dexterity or coordination especially in the execution of learned physical tasks; a learned power of doing something competently : a developed aptitude or ability

❋ owl thinking/wise mind thinking-wise mind is that place where reasonable mind and emotional mind come together; it is the integration of both

❋ persistence-to go on resolutely or stubbornly in spite of opposition; or beyond the self-talk

❋ physiology-of or relating to the body

❋ refocus-to change the emphasis or direction of any negative direction or thinking

❋ relaxed breathing-technique that helps you slow down your breathing when feeling stressed or anxious

❋ shaping-to modify (behavior) by rewarding changes that tend toward a desired response;

❋ shaping changes in positions toward mastery

❋ skill mastery-having the ability to perform a task flowingly

❋ special events in your family-rituals that make you feel connected and together

❋ thinking informs our bodies-how you think is how you feel; your body feels your thoughts

❋ visualization-the act or process of interpreting in visual terms or of putting into visible form; formation of mental visual images

❋ word and deed-alignment of espoused ideas and follow through with action steps

Definitions: 2018 Merriam-Webster online, Incorporated

Be your best and chivalry in action

Printed in the United States
By Bookmasters